Angels Sweep the Desert Floor

Angels Sweep the Desert Floor

Bible Legends About Moses in the Wilderness

MIRIAM CHAIKIN • Illustrated by ALEXANDER KOSHKIN

CLARION BOOKS • New York

Clarion Books
a Houghton Mifflin Company imprint
215 Park Avenue South, New York, NY 10003
Text copyright © 2002 by Miriam Chaikin
Illustrations copyright © 2002 by Alexander Koshkin

The illustrations were executed in watercolor, tempera, and gouache on Gosznac paper.
The text was set in 14-point Goudy.

Book design by Patrice Sheridan.

www.houghtonmifflinbooks.com

Printed in Singapore

Library of Congress Cataloging-in-Publication Data
Chaikin, Miriam.
Angels sweep the desert floor: Bible legends about Moses in the
wilderness / by Miriam Chaikin ; illustrated by Alexander Koshkin.
p.   cm.
Includes bibliographical references.
Summary: A collection of eighteen stories based on the Bible which
tell how angels respond to God's commands to ease the way for Moses
and the Israelites as they cross the wilderness after being freed from
slavery in Egypt.
ISBN 0-395-97825-4
1. Moses (Biblical leader)—Juvenile literature. 2. Angels (Judaism)—Juvenile literature.
3. Legends, Jewish. 4. Midrash—Juvenile literature. 5. Bible. O. T. Pentateuch—Legends.
[1. Moses (Biblical leader). 2. Angels. 3. Jews—Folklore. 4. Midrash.
5. Bible. O. T. Exodus.] I. Koshkin, Alexander, ill. II. Title.

BS580.M6 C43 2002
296.1'42—dc21

2001047501

TWP 10 9 8 7 6 5 4 3 2 1

To the new branch on the family tree,

Julie Chaikin Pearl & Fred Colman

—M. C.

To the memory of my mother

—A. K.

Contents

Contents

Introduction

The language of the Bible is beautiful and precise. What is said is clear. But there are gaps in stories. Information is missing.

Ancient rabbis believed that the answers to all questions could be found in the Bible, that one has only to search its pages. Their motto was "Turn it and turn it, for everything is in it."

The Creation story provides an example. God creates the world and fills it with earth, sky, lands, seas, and animals. Then God says, "Let us make humans in our image." But to whom was God talking? He has thus far made only places and animals. Here is a gap. Information is missing.

Rabbis searched the pages for possible answers. As animals had already been created, one rabbi said, "God was talking to the animals."

A second rabbi found another answer. He noticed that while angels do not appear on the list of things created, they do appear in Bible stories. Angels visit Abraham. Elsewhere, God says to Moses, "My angel shall go before you." The prophet Zechariah told the people, *"Some angels walk to and fro on earth."*

The second rabbi, reasoning that not everything created was named at Creation, said, "God was talking to the angels."

Angels became a subject for discussion. What were they, exactly, these angels? A biblical psalm says: *"Bless the Lord, all you his angels, you mighty in strength, who do his bidding, obeying his spoken word."* This suggests that angels are God's messengers, his servants.

Reading on, the rabbis found more kinds of angels. The prophet Isaiah, in a vision of heaven, says he heard "angels singing *Holy, holy, holy, the whole world is full of his glory*" before God.

There were also guardian angels. Didn't God send an angel to protect Moses? The psalmists also speak of guardian angels: *The Lord shall preserve your going out and coming in. He will give his angels charge over you to keep you in all your ways.*

The prophet Isaiah speaks of seraphim. This class of angels hovered about the celestial throne. Each had six wings: two covered the face, two covered the feet, two were for flying.

Biblical poets, the psalm writers, spoke of angels as messengers and ministers, saying, "God makes the winds his messengers and flaming fire his ministers."

The Bible speaks of cherubim, a class of angels stationed at the Garden of Eden, armed with flaming swords to keep anyone from entering. In legend they are winged beings that guard sacred places.

Messenger angels, angels who walk the earth, singing angels, guardians, ministers: Where are they all, these different angels?

Isaiah, in his vision of heaven, said the angel choir sang before God. So they were in the presence of God.

But where is God? And where is heaven?

Searching, explaining, interpreting, rabbis and biblical poets formed the view that God created two worlds, one below, for us, his creatures, and one above, for himself and his angels. They saw the upper world as God's kingdom, a heavenly court "full of the brightness of the Lord's glory," a vast, vast region consisting of seven heavens and containing untold millions of angels, with God, hidden by a white curtain, in the highest heaven.

The rabbis discussed and reasoned and came to the belief that the two worlds were linked. Would God create a world below, fill it with marvels, and then turn away from it? It did not seem likely. What seemed more likely was that God felt he had done his part, creating a beautiful world, and that it was now up to his humans to improve the world, make it better.

There is also evidence in the Bible of God's presence in this world. Though invisible, did not God speak to the people of the Bible? And did he not hold conversations with Moses? And order Moses back to Egypt to free the Israelite slaves? And tell Moses not to worry about what words to speak to the pharaoh, saying, "I will be with your mouth and tell you what to say"?

God also spoke to the biblical prophets, who repeated God's word to the people. The prophet Isaiah, speaking for God, said to the Israelites, *"Heaven is my throne, and the earth is my footstool."* The prophet Ezekiel told them, *"Ye my flock, the flock of my pasture, are humans, and I am your God."*

Moses taught the Israelites, "God is God above and below." King David, praising God, echoed the thought, saying, "All in heaven and earth is yours."

Biblical poets, the psalm writers, added to the idea of God's presence in both worlds, saying, *"God is king of all the earth."* And *"The Lord looked down from heaven."*

Rabbis, seeking to draw closer to God, saw God's presence in both worlds as a link between the two worlds. They saw miracles, which only God can create, as a manifestation of God's presence in this world—a link. Angels who go back and forth between earth and heaven were another link. The guardian angel that God sent to Moses in the wilderness was a clear link.

Considering the matter, the rabbis believed that a loving God was not likely to create one or two guardian angels and stop there. God's compassionate nature would lead him to create myriads of guardian angels, enough so there would be one for each good human on earth, creating ever more links between the two worlds.

Some rabbis went deeper. They saw a link in the seed that mysteriously becomes a plant, in rain that falls in just the right amount to water the earth so food will grow. It seemed that God created guardian angels not only for each human but for each thing on earth. As one rabbi put it, "Each individual blade of grass has a guardian of its own, telling it how to grow."

Books seemed to be another link between the two worlds. For God in heaven tells the prophets Isaiah and Jeremiah what to write in their books and commands Moses what to write in his book, saying, "Write you this song" and "Write this for a memorial in the book."

The Bible tells us that books were also written in heaven. Moses, in a moment of anger, asks God to erase his name, saying, "I pray you, blot me out of your book."

And who wrote these books in heaven? Ancient rabbis had an answer. As books on earth were then written by scribes—secretaries—so were there angel scribes to write books in heaven. Yet another class of angels.

Each answer the rabbis found became a type of story called a *Midrash* (*Midrashim* in the plural), a Hebrew word that means "search [the Bible] and explain." Each *Midrash* was a building block for another *Midrash*, or story. Rabbis used a *Midrash* in their sermons, to teach their students, and to explain biblical passages to the people. They added details of local color, creating yet other stories. Storytellers created stories based on *Midrashim*, introducing elements of their own to enliven the telling.

In this way there arose over the ages an enormous body of Bible-based Jewish literature consisting of *Midrashim*, folktales, and imaginative legends. Whatever label the stories wear, all have one aim in common: to bring God closer to people and people closer to God. As the rabbis would put it, to link the soul of the individual with God.

The stories in this book link the world above with the world below. They are set in heaven, in God's luminous court, where myriads of angels fly about carrying out God's commands, some more eagerly than others. They are also set in the desert wilderness, where God sends angels to ease the way for Moses and the Israelites. The stories are based on existing Bible legends and begin not when Moses is sent to Egypt to free the slaves but after he has freed them, when they wander in the wilderness.

As the stories begin and we join Moses and the Israelites, Moses goes from his tent with the rod he used to perform miracles before the Egyptian pharaoh. The rod is sacred. It is inscribed with the secret name of God. The Hebrew letters representing God's secret name are YUD HEY VAV HEY. In English, YHVH. *Ya* is a known name of God in the Bible. *El* is another. The rabbis, assigning in their stories duties to angels, gave them names ending with the sound *el*, linking them to God.

In legend, the rod Moses carried was inscribed by the celestial scribe Ya'asriel, angel of the seventy pencils.

I

The Sacred Rod

As night drew to a close in the desert wilderness, life began to stir in the Israelite camp. Moses had been awake for some time. He raised the flap of his tent and looked out. Dawn was spreading pink banners on the horizon. He took up the sacred rod and went from the tent. Just touching the rod, taking it up, sent a surge of strength through his body. Small wonder. It was inscribed with God's secret name. From that the rod drew its power.

Moses thought of the Egyptian pharaoh as he walked through the camp, past rows of tents, past the animals—donkeys, camels, goats, sheep. How the pharaoh had mocked the idea of God. Asked his courtiers, sneering, if any among them had ever heard of this God of the Israelites. He soon learned about God. With the rod, Moses had performed fearful deeds in Egypt, worked miracles and marvels. In the end the pharaoh bowed to God's superior power. He freed the Israelite slaves, let them go.

The miracles and marvels Moses had performed were not meant only to impress Egyptians. They were meant to move the hearts of Israelites as well. The people had been slaves for too long and had forgotten God. They thought only of filling their bellies, the endless toil they had endured, and their weary bones.

A sheep bleated as Moses turned up another lane of tents, reminding him how his life had changed since his days as a shepherd. He had taken his sheep out to graze in the wilderness. As he leaned against a boulder, idly watching them, he saw a remarkable sight. A thornbush was on fire. It burned and burned, yet it remained whole. He walked up to the bush for a closer look and saw an angel in the flame, and heard God's voice tell him to go to Egypt to free the Israelite slaves.

Moses shook his head at the memory, still unable to believe his response. He had refused to go. Refused to obey God. He had made excuses for himself, saying he had a thick tongue and was a poor speaker, that it would be shameful for a tongue-tied man to represent God before the pharaoh. It availed him nothing. God had turned away each excuse. Moses was ordered to take his brother Aaron to speak for him.

Sleepy voices came from the tents. Moses glanced about. They were a mixed lot, his people. Some were Israelites, some Egyptians, some members of other tribes who had joined them. They were all one now, whatever their origin. They were Israelites, a free people. Or so it was thought. They were free but not yet a people.

God had ordered Moses to mold them into a nation that worshiped God and bring them to the land of milk and honey God had set aside for them. It was not an easy task. A nation believed and thought with one mind.

How many evenings, sitting around the fire, had he—or his brother Aaron—or his sister Miriam—tried to teach the people the greatness of God?

"God made the whole world and everything in it," they explained.

The people could not grasp the idea. "In Egypt we could see gods. Why can't we see this God?"

"God is invisible," they said. "You cannot see God. You can only know God through his greatness."

"Where is the greatness?"

"Look about you. See the marvels God has put into the world," Moses would say. "Desert sands, seasons, the sun, moon, and stars that decorate heaven. Is this not something to wonder at?"

The people did wonder, but not about God. They wondered when it would be time to eat again. And how much longer the food they had brought from Egypt would last.

Moses rapped lightly on Aaron's tent in greeting. Aaron lifted the door flap and stepped outside. The brothers took each other by the elbow and touched cheeks. Moses glanced over Aaron's shoulder and saw inside the tent Aaron's sons rolling up sleeping mats, bundling robes, and packing eating utensils.

Moses greets Aaron.

"Good morning, Moses," a woman's voice called.

Both brothers turned. Miriam, their sister, appeared as her tent was low-ered. Caleb, her husband, stood folding it. Moses raised a hand in greeting. Miriam, his older sister, had been a second mother to him.

"You are deeper into the day than we are," Moses said.

"Let it be an example to the people," Caleb called.

Miriam lifted bundles onto the back of a waiting donkey. Moses could hear from the clink of metal disks that her tambourine had been packed.

"Daylight already creeps along the desert floor," she said.

2

The World Above, the World Below

In God's kingdom of seven heavens time does not exist. There is no night, no day, no early or late. Angels move always and always in a glorious amber light. It is the light of God's glory radiating out from behind the Holy Curtain that hides God.

In the world below, which the Holy One—as the angels call God—had made for his earth creatures, time does exist. The Holy One had put lights in the sky to separate the night from the day.

The order that time worked on earth pleased the Holy One. He liked the harmony of movement—people rising at dawn, feeding their animals, feeding themselves, conversing with each other, finding amusement, preparing for sleep. To create another link between his world and the one below, he ordered the angels to connect their duties to the earth day. And when morning came for Moses and the Israelites in the desert wilderness, to think of it as morning in heaven, too.

Thus it was that as Moses walked through the Israelite camp at dawn on earth, in heaven the angel choir and angel musicians were gathering for morning hymns. Making harp and bell sounds with their lips, musicians accompanied the choir singing the first morning hymn: *"Holy, holy, holy is God. The whole world is full of his glory."*

When the morning round of hymn singing was over, the younger angels became astir with excitement. They were eager to see the sight that awaited them on earth. But first they would fly up to the seventh heaven to kiss the nearness of Glory. They could not see the Holy One. No angel could. He was hidden by the Holy Curtain. They could have kissed the amber light of Glory wherever they were, for it filled all heavens. But that would not do. The young angels believed the closer to the Curtain they came, the greater portion of bliss would be theirs.

Up they flew, past the storerooms of Ya'asriel, angel of the seventy pencils, past the chambers of the fiery sparks, past the secret quarters of the glowing wheels, past the gates of the guardians, past the troops of wrath and destruction, past myriads of helper angels, on up to the seventh heaven. Thousands of seraphim surrounded the Holy Curtain and the archangels together with their battalions hovered about. The young angels had no difficulty in drawing close to the Curtain. Crowding is unknown in heaven. As angels gather, space opens to receive all comers. The young angels approached the Curtain and, basking in bliss, spoke words of love to the Holy One.

Filled with happiness, they left the precincts of the seventh heaven and flew down, calling as they went, "Come and see." In each heaven they passed they were joined by more and more young angels.

And what was it that they were so eager to see?

From the time that they had been created, they loved to watch the play of light on earth, to see darkness leave the desert floor and daylight roll in. The sight enchanted them. Ever since the Holy One had drawn Moses into his plans, they had even more to enjoy. They had been following the movements of the Israelites from the time they left Egypt. The sight made for a colorful spectacle in the barren desert wilderness.

The angels took their places at the heavenly viewing stand. The Israelites had broken camp and were forming a line to march, family by family, pack animals beside them, little ones on the backs of donkeys. The angels looked over the line of marchers. They saw in the lead Moses' brother Aaron and his family and Moses' sister Miriam and her family. But where was Moses?

They did not wonder about Moses long, for they were easily distracted. The length of the line had captured their attention.

"It covers eighteen miles of ground," said an angel.

"There are six hundred thousand of them," said another.

"Angels!" God's voice said.

The angels hearkened. "Holiness?" they asked, waiting to hear what was wanted.

"They are not for counting. The sun beats down on them. It will soon release its fiery breath. Go down and ease their way."

Young angels did not like to leave heaven. No angel did. Being away from God's glory meant being separated from bliss, from happiness. No angel could bear to be away from heaven for long. But the Holy One had spoken. And the angels obeyed.

Making themselves invisible, the flap of wings heard only by themselves, a band of seven hundred twenty young angels flew down, plucking clouds from the sky as they went, sped on their way by a hunger to return to the precincts of Glory.

3

Gifts in the Wilderness

The angels had strung clouds together into a vast sheet and made cloud tassels to hang from the edges. And before the rising sun could release its greatest heat, they spread a canopy of clouds over the marchers, providing them with shade.

"Done," said an angel, anxious to get back to heaven. "We have eased their way. We may return."

"Not yet," said another. "We can do more."

Nothing more needed to be said. The same thought formed in the mind of each angel. Angels on a mission for the Holy One can change themselves into anything, take on any shape, to accomplish a task. Without exchanging a word, they divided themselves into two groups.

One group turned itself into a pleasant breeze and went to play up and down the line of marchers, up and down, cooling them, bringing comfort.

The second group became sucking, sweeping things. Hurling themselves over the desert floor, they cleared away all biting creatures, large and small. When they were through, they had removed from the land lizards, scorpions, and all harmful creatures except one—the red-eyed monster. This deadly snake can kill a bird flying overhead just by moving over its shadow. The angels had to see the monster to get rid of him. And he was in hiding.

"In the Book of Secrets in Ya'asriel's library I read that the red-eyed monster relishes the taste of crows," said an angel. "I know how to fool him."

She turned herself into a crow and flew round and about, round and about. Under the boulder where the monster lay coiled, a red eye grew large with malice. Recognizing the shadow of a crow, the monster crawled out, its flame eye blinking and flashing. The angel had planned well. Before the monster could reach the shadow, the crow angel changed herself into an ibis, a gentle bird with long legs and a curved beak. The angel knew from the Book of Secrets that the sight of an ibis causes the deadly snake to perish.

These gifts—shade, a breeze, and a safe desert floor—were not the only ones the Holy One had bestowed upon the Israelites. From the day they left Egypt, they had not known hunger, for the Holy One had created just for them

Angels bring gifts to the Israelites.

a mill in the third heaven, along with a class of baker angels. The bakers baked all night and in the morning rained down on the Israelite camp great quantities of manna, enough for every family.

Manna was more than a source of nourishment. It was a wonder food. In each mouth it tasted like a favorite food. To infants it tasted like milk. To young people, like fresh-baked bread. Old people found in it the taste of honey and milk. The sick, when they ate it, thought they were eating barley with oil and honey.

Manna was also fragrant, releasing a lovely aroma into the air as it fell.

The angels looked over the line of marchers, pleased with their day's work.

"Come, let us return," said an angel.

"Our work is not yet over," said a voice the angels did not recognize. They turned and saw an angel they had not seen before.

"You are new," said one.

"Yes, created this morning," the new angel answered.

"What else can we do for them?" the angels asked.

"What is the most precious thing in a dry desert—more precious than rubies?" she asked in reply.

"Water is more precious than rubies," the angels answered with one voice, surprised they hadn't thought of it themselves.

"The water bags they brought with them from Egypt will soon be empty," the new angel said.

All the angels agreed that water should be provided for the Israelites. But how should it be done?

"If they were settled, we could create a well," said an angel.

"But they are not settled," said another. "They wander from place to place."

"And will continue to wander, until they reach the river Jordan," said a third.

"We are not thinking like angels," said the new angel.

The others turned to her.

"The Holy One wants us to act like him, imitate him, be creative," she said.

"We have created shade, a breeze, a clean desert floor this very day," said an angel. "What can we create in this instance?"

"A well that wanders with them," the new angel said.

The angels seized upon the idea enthusiastically. They tore a jagged boulder from its mates. Releasing their hands, which they kept tucked under their wings, they circled the rock and circled it, applying small slaps as they went, flattening corners, patting down surfaces, making them smooth. Before long, the jagged boulder was as round as a moon. With their fingers the angels poked holes in the rock, making outlets for water. Gathering around the rock, standing wing to wing, they filled it with a never-ending supply of water.

"A perfect time to receive a gift," said an angel.

The angels glanced at the line of marchers and saw Aaron, who was at the front of the line, raise his banner, signaling the marchers to come to a halt. Mothers removed their little ones from the backs of donkeys, young children began at once to hop about and play, fathers went to feed the animals.

As Aaron turned to speak to his sister Miriam, the angels formed a group behind the rock and rolled it across the desert floor.

4

The Miriam Well

As the Israelites were settling themselves, their little ones, and their animals, they saw a large rock rolling toward them. They knew it was a gift from God. So did God's gifts come to them, suddenly and seemingly from nowhere. Like the manna. Like the shade. But this rock, what was it for? They walked around the rock, inspecting it.

Angels had spoken to Aaron before. He could not see them, they were invisible, but he could hear them. He tilted his head to listen and heard an angel voice telling him how the rock was to be used. Miriam, sitting nearby, knew from the expression on her brother's face that he was listening to angels. Wondering what he had heard, she rose from her place and went up to her brother.

"Come with me," he said.

The two walked up to the rock, and Aaron laid a hand on it.

Miriam sings, praising God.

"Spring up, O well," he said.

At his words, water began to trickle out. When the people saw the precious water they ran, each to a spout, drinking joyously, holding up their little ones to sip from the well. They filled their jugs with water, then brought their animals to drink.

Miriam saw the joy of the people. "We must thank God for the gift of water," she said. And she took up her tambourine and began a song of praise, singing, *"Sing a song to God, for he is great, he is mighty."* Young men and women took up their lutes and pipes and played as the women stopped what they were doing and came to sing and dance with her.

The angels watched with satisfaction. Their work was over. They were free to go. But how could they leave while songs of praise were being sung to the Holy One?

Aaron touched the rock, and the water ceased to flow.

The people looked up to Miriam and loved her. They called her Prophet.

"Miriam," one called. "You often speak to us about the closeness of heaven and earth and the links that connect them. These gifts we receive, are they links?"

"They are gifts of God's caring, not links," she said. "The manna, the well—this rock—they will be gone when our journey is over. A link is forever."

"Like the blade of grass and its guardian?" someone asked.

"Like that," Miriam said. "The link between the blade of grass and its guardian angel is forever."

The younger angels were not guardians. But it pleased them to learn that the Holy One's plan was understood on earth.

"You have said the grasses sing a song of praise to God," the children said. "How do you know? Can you hear it?"

"I can, sometimes," Miriam said.

"Sing it for us," the children said.

"I cannot sing their song. It belongs to them," Miriam said. "I can only sing my song." And closing her eyes, the better to be alone with the words, she sang:

"Each blade of grass
sings a song of praise
to the Holy One.
How lovely their song.
How good to worship
with them."

At the end of her song someone called, "This gift, this rock, must have a name. What should it be?"

The angels were in a dilemma. They wanted to return to heaven, but they were also curious to learn what name the rock would receive.

The women began a naming ceremony, asking questions for others to answer.

"Who saved the infant Moses?"

"Miriam, his sister, she did."

"If not for Miriam, would we have Moses?"

"We would not."

Men and women asked together, "And if we did not have Moses, where would we be?" They turned to Aaron to finish.

"We would still be slaves in Egypt."

"The Miriam Well!" the people shouted with one voice. "That is the name of the rock."

The angels saw the glad hearts of the Israelites and longed for their own source of happiness—the amber rays of Glory that glowed from the Holy Curtain. Spreading their wings, they flew up singing their song of return, *"Our one desire is to be beside you, beside you we have no desire."*

5

By the Mouth of the Cloud

And where was Moses?

It happens that as the angels went down to ease the way for the Israelites, the Holy One called Moses to come up.

Moses had been up before. The angels knew him. They had taught him secrets. Hearing the call, Moses moved away from Aaron, Miriam, and the elders and spoke the words "I am here."

A large gray cloud appeared and opened its mouth. Moses stepped inside, as if into a room, and was carried up to the first heaven. There he was transformed into an angel and could rise up on his own.

As he ascended, the Sour Faces placed themselves before him, blocking his way.

Moses knew these Sour Faces. They were left over from the time archangel Satan tried to stop God from creating humans. Satan was jealous. He was afraid

God might come to love humans more than he loved angels. And he went from heaven to heaven spreading bad words, until the Holy One expelled him and his followers.

The Holy One relented and allowed a few weak-willed followers of Satan to remain. The Sour Faces were not among the agitators. They had only trailed after Satan, saying nothing. While they were permitted to stay, they had lost their angel natures. They were no longer beautiful, loving, sunny beings. They were cranky and jealous. That is how they came by the name Sour Faces. Other angels avoided them.

"You are human, born of woman," the Sour Faces said to Moses. "What right have you in this holy place?"

Moses had dealt with them before. He drew on his patience. "The Holy One has sent for me to come up," he said.

The voice of the Holy One now spoke harshly to the Sour Faces. "You have been troublesome from the beginning," he said. And he sent for the highest angel, Metatron, prince of the Face, an angel who had been born human and on earth was known as Enoch.

"Bring Moses up," the Holy One said.

Metatron scolded the Sour Faces. "A meanness clings to you from the time you supported the Alien," he said. So did the angels call Satan, rather than speak the hateful name.

"We did not support him. We only listened," the Sour Faces said.

"And for that reason you were spared and not cast out of heaven," Metatron said. "But you are not lovable."

The Sour Faces knew they were little loved. They knew other angels called them not only Sour Faces but also "little aliens."

Moses and Metatron rose up, greeting and being greeted by the myriads of angels they passed on their way through the forty-nine gates of wisdom. There were, in all, fifty gates. The fiftieth gate was sealed. Angels pass it as they go to and fro and do not know what it is, or even that it is a gate. Metatron and angel Raziel, who sits outside the Holy Curtain, know it is there. But no one, *no one*—not even they, high angels though they are—may enter.

Metatron paused at the gate of the guardian angels. "The Holy One loves all his angels, and especially these, the guardians, his links to earth," he said to Moses.

Moses' own guardian was Micha'el. She watched over him, guiding his steps, keeping him from harm. Sometimes he could feel her breath on the back of his neck.

Behind the gate Moses could hear tree guardians speaking to their earth links. Carob tree guardians were telling their trees when to put forth fruit. Palm and pistachio guardians were instructing their links when to flower, when to

Moses is called to heaven.

seed. Guardians of the willow tree and hyssop bush passed on healing secrets to their links.

Moses paused before an empty gate. He saw no one and nothing inside. But the aroma that came from there was so fragrant, so pleasing, he could not move from the spot.

"It is the fragrance of the apple orchard," Metatron said. "When the Shekina goes down, the fragrance accompanies her."

Moses understood. God does not leave heaven. The Shekina, God's female presence on earth, goes down for him. She appears as an amber glow. When God's glory appears on earth, it is the Shekina. When God speaks on earth, her voice is heard.

Metatron and Moses continued upward, passing Rahmiel, angel of mercy, Tsadkiel, angel of justice, and myriads of angels busy at their tasks. In the seventh heaven Metatron disappeared from Moses' side, and Moses stood alone on a point of light, the tip of a blinding spark of beauty that radiated out from the Holy Curtain. Around him the voices of the great Heavenly Choir rose up singing with surpassing sweetness, *"Enter his gates with thanksgiving, his courts with praise."*

6

Angel Raziel

Angel Raziel, in her place outside the Holy Curtain, watched Moses arrive. Her constant nearness to the Holy One placed her just after Metatron in importance. Her name means, "hears God's secrets."

"Approach, Moses," she said.

Moses drifted freely in a blissful state through an amber golden haze toward the Holy Curtain.

A voice like sweet rushing waters spoke.

"Moses," the Holy One said, "I have created humans in my image. I have called you up to put before them this proposal. The world I have created for them is a great and good world, a world of plenty. I would like now to see them improve the world, make it better. Here are Ten Pathways for them to follow. If they accept, I will come down in three days and claim them for my own. They will be my people and I will be their God."

Raziel, listening with Moses, heard the Holy One recite the Ten Pathways:

"I am the Lord your God who brought you out of Egypt to be your God.

"You shall have no other gods beside me.

"Do not make false vows in my name.

"Remember the Sabbath day to keep it holy.

"Honor your father and mother.

"Do not murder.

"Do not commit adultery.

"Do not steal.

"Do not tell lies.

"Do not crave your neighbor's possessions."

Moses would obey the Holy One without question. And he would do so now. But this was a complicated task. He needed guidance. How to ask for it?

"Great and Holy One," he said. "The people are simple. They ask me who you are, and I try to tell them. I say, 'Study God's great works and you will know his greatness.' They ask, 'Which great works?' I say, 'The world around you—the lands and seas, the sun, moon, and stars.' They do not grasp the idea. Aaron says the same to them in his words. Miriam teaches them in her words. The people are slow to understand."

"Speak plainly, Moses," the Holy One said.

To speak plainly was what Moses had been trying not to do. To speak plainly he would have to say the Israelites did not appreciate all that the Holy One had done for them. That they were ungrateful and full of complaints. Moses thought it would pain the Holy One to hear this. He spoke as plainly as circumstances allowed.

"When I put the Ten Pathways before them, they will want to know what you will do for them in return," he said.

Angel Raziel, at the Holy Curtain, could hardly keep from laughing.

"In return?" the Holy One said. "The pathways are for *their* good, not mine. If they follow them, their hearts will be at peace. They will be free of guilt or shame. Their eyes will open to the marvels I have made for their enjoyment. They will be well off."

Moses knew the people. He proceeded carefully. "Great and Holy One," he said. "They will want to know what you mean by 'well off.'"

"Tell them," the Holy One said, "that the land I am giving them is a good land. That I will send rain to water their crops so that they will have figs, dates, grains, wine, and oil in season. They will eat and be satisfied. Their animals also. Tell them I will keep enemies away from their door."

The Holy One stopped speaking. Raziel turned her face toward the Holy Curtain. Moses understood his interview was over. He would have liked to stay on, speaking, but found himself unwillingly drifting away.

"Moses," the Holy One called after him. "Repeat the pathways exactly as I have given them to you. Add no word, subtract none. If the Israelites accept, I will come down on the mount to meet them in three days."

7

Moses Silences the Angels

On his way down, the Sour Faces once more stopped Moses.

"We overheard the Holy One give you something," they said. "What was it?"

They had no right to ask. Moses did not have to answer. But the glow of Glory was yet upon him and he was full of love.

"The Holy One has given me Ten Pathways for the Israelites," he said.

"Ten?" the angels repeated. They did not know what the pathways were. But that Moses had received not one but ten rankled them.

"We were created before you humans," they said. "The pathways should have been given to us, celestial beings, not to dwellers of the dust."

"They apply to humans, not to you," Moses said.

"To us," the angels repeated, flapping their wings in agitation.

Moses reasoned with them. "Here are some pathways. Decide for yourselves," he said. And he repeated: "'I am the Lord your God who brought you out of Egypt to be your God. You shall have no other god beside me.'"

He paused. "Were you slaves in Egypt?" he asked. "Would you worship some handmade god that people often worship, rather than the living God who made you?"

The angels made sniffling noises, which Moses took to mean "No."

"Would you make false vows in God's name? Might you swear falsely?" Moses asked.

The idea made the Sour Faces smile. Angels were incapable of such a thing.

Moses continued. "'Remember the Sabbath day to keep it holy,'" he said. "Is this something for you?"

"There is no time in heaven," they said sharply, sensing that they were going to be proved wrong. "No seventh day. There is always and always only a golden holiness."

As Moses spoke on, the angels felt more and more foolish. Moses had spoken truly: The pathways were meant for humans, not angels.

"Forgive us, Moses," they said.

Moses and the Sour Faces.

The sincerity of their apology drove out their crankiness, and love began to flow from them, sweetening their faces.

"Consider us your loving friends," they said.

The large gray cloud that had taken Moses up now appeared to take him down. And as he stepped inside, the once Sour Faces showered him with kisses.

8

Something Entirely New

When the angels who had eased the way for the Israelites returned from the desert wilderness, Moses was yet in heaven. The angels had no way of knowing this. They had not passed the great cloud that had carried Moses up. Nor would they have seen it. Heaven is vast. So vast, a ten-mile band of angels can fly alongside another ten-mile band of angels without the two groups seeing each other. So vast, a human would have to walk five hundred years to go from one end to the other, and then walk another five hundred years to go from the uppermost to the lowest part.

The angels on the way up were too full of longing for the glow of Glory to notice anything. When they arrived in heaven, they knew the Holy One was speaking with someone. They heard the Heavenly Choir singing. The singing in itself meant nothing. The choir sang all the time, with words. Now they sang a wordless melody, making sweet sounds with their lips. Also, Raziel sat with her ear to the Holy Curtain.

She was not eavesdropping. God forbid. Stationed outside the Holy Curtain, she hears the Holy One's conversations. If what she hears is a secret that belongs to heaven, she keeps it to herself. But if the subject involves humans, she passes the news on to the other angels. And this she did now.

"Angels," she said. "You will want to hear this. The Holy One has just finished speaking with Moses."

The angels who had returned from the wilderness realized only now that they had not seen Moses below.

"That explains why he was not with his brother and sister and the others," said an angel.

The angels were not surprised by Moses' presence in heaven. They had seen him there before. Each time he had been called up for a reason. What was the reason this time?

"The Holy One is about to do something new," Raziel said. "Something that has never been done before."

The angels, curious, fluttered their wings in excitement.

"With how many humans has the Holy One spoken since he created the world?" Raziel asked.

"Very few," said an angel.

"Three—" said another.

"Four?" asked yet another.

"In three days' time," Raziel continued, "the Holy One will go down to speak with the Israelites, with all of them at once—men, women, children."

"All the people?" the angels asked with one voice.

"All," Raziel repeated.

"To speak about what?" said another.

"The Holy One will appear on a mount and offer the Israelites Ten Pathways," Raziel said. "If they accept, he will claim them for his own."

The angels were full of wonder.

"That is certainly something that has never been done before," said one.

"Let us hope the Alien does not hear of it," Raziel said.

"He won't," said Ya'asriel, angel of the seventy pencils. "The Holy One has sent him on an errand. I myself wrote the order."

The angels tittered. Although Satan was not allowed to set foot in heaven, the Holy One sent him on an errand to the north from time to time, to get him out of the way.

Ya'asriel continued, "The order reads so: *In the north are those whose feet rush to do evil, who lie, cheat, and act cruelly. Torment them. If they repent, cease the torments. If they continue, devise harsher torments.*"

Abraziel, keeper of the gates, spoke up. "I have seen those people," he said. "They are fixed in their ways and will not soon repent."

"Of course not," said a ministering angel. "That is why the Holy One sent the Alien there. So he will be kept good and busy by his work."

Raziel, usually proper and dignified, laughed. The angels hovering nearby joined in, and as the news spread, the tinkle of angel laughter filled all heavens.

9

The Mountains Argue

The angels became aware of a commotion on Earth and looked to see what it was. The mountains, usually silent and still, were stirring.

"What is it?" asked an angel.

"They are arguing," Raziel said. "They heard me say the Holy One will appear on a mount. Each one thinks of itself as the chosen mount. Just listen to them . . ."

"I am the only possible choice," said Mount Carmel. "I am as wide as I am handsome. I straddle the Holy One's great creations and have one foot on land, the other in the sea."

Mount Hermon, a tall, imposing mountain in the north, shook with indignation, loosening the patches of late snow that clung to her shoulders. "I am larger than you. The honor will be mine," she said.

The mountains argue.

"What has size to do with it?" said Mount Tabor. "Beauty is everything, and I am the most beautiful. Flowers and plants cover my perfect dome."

Raziel lost patience with them. "Oh, you fools in the world!" she said. "You mountains are among the oldest creations. You have been in the world longer than almost anything. Yet you haven't learned even what the lowly locust knows: Your Maker hates quarreling. He detests boasting and jealousy. Why would he choose any of you?"

The mountains fell silent.

Raziel continued. "While you were bragging, little Mount Sinai spoke not a word," she said. "Sinai was as silent as the wilderness around her. Learn something from her. She has no distinguishing features except one—she is modest. That is a quality the Holy One loves greatly. He will appear on Sinai."

The mountains looked heavily away, disappointed. Raziel felt sorry for them and smoothed over their feelings.

"Sinai has been chosen for another reason as well," she said. "You mountains are all in Israel. She is outside, in the wilderness, in no-man's-land. If the Holy One appeared on any of you, people would say, 'The Ten Pathways were given in Israel. They are meant for Israelites, not for us.' They would then have an excuse to behave badly."

The mountains, content, settled back into their former calm.

10

Satan Tries to Interfere

The angels were sure Satan had enough to do in the north to keep him occupied for days on end. They should have known better. Satan is clever, he is canny, and he is easily bored.

He threw himself into the task, visiting on the wicked people of the north harsh torments, relishing every new agony he devised. But they had no effect. The people took great delight in wickedness. They laughed at Satan's torments. They did not repent. In fact, they grew bolder and committed even more wicked acts shamelessly in public, out in the open, for all to see.

Satan grew bored with their games and changed his tactics. He took advantage of their greed and filled the mouths of caves with sparkle and glitter and spread shiny stuff over the floors. With tricks and enticements, he lured the people to the caves. When they were well inside, searching for treasure, he made gates of wasps and laid them over the entrances, leaving the greedy to share the cave with bats, scorpions, and horrible creatures they never knew existed. In a few days, he reasoned, he would return, at which time they would be more than willing to repent.

Satisfied with his solution to the problem, Satan went in search of some employment for himself. Thus it was that he flew over the mountains and heard them arguing, heard Raziel chastise them, and learned that the Holy One was going down to meet the Israelites and claim them for his own. The idea riled him. He was eaten up with jealousy.

As an angel in disgrace, Satan could not enter the holy precincts of heaven. But as an angel, he had the right to speak to God from a distance.

"Great and all-powerful One, may I be heard?" Satan asked.

Raziel, from her place outside the Holy Curtain, was startled to hear Satan's detestable voice. She loved the Holy One's kindness but thought he had gone too far in allowing the Alien to speak to him.

News travels quickly in heaven. Angels who were free of duties came flying to the Holy Curtain from all directions. They could not hear the conversation between the Holy One and Satan, but Raziel would repeat it to them when it was over.

"Great and all-powerful One," Satan said. "I have learned of your plan to go down to meet the Israelites."

"What concern is it of yours?"

"My concern is for you," Satan said.

Raziel winced.

"For me?" the Holy One said.

"You have had nothing but heartache from humans," Satan said. "I do not want to see you hurt again."

Raziel could barely contain herself.

"Your first creations, Adam and Eve, disappointed you," Satan continued. "Their descendants disappointed you. The descendants of Noah and Naamah, whom you saved from the flood, disappointed you. Now you plan to meet and claim for your own these Israelites, who worshiped rams in Egypt? Who took on foreign ways to pass as Egyptians?"

"They act according to their natures. I act according to mine," the Holy One said.

Raziel smiled at the Holy One's answer.

"They doubted that you exist," Satan continued. "You had to perform miracles for them to prove that you do. They are fickle-hearted. And you are going to claim them for your own, make them your people?"

"You have done worse, and I let you speak to me," the Holy One said.

Raziel covered her mouth to keep from laughing. From the silence that followed, she knew the interview was over. She turned to the waiting angels and, as she told them what had been said, enjoyed the conversation for a second time.

Raziel listens at the Holy Curtain as Satan speaks to God.

II

But Do You See God?

In the Israelite camp the people awaited with eagerness—and some trepidation—the return of Moses, their leader. God had spoken to them through Moses before. And Moses had again gone to speak with God. What would God have to say to them this time?

When Moses reappeared in the camp, he was radiant. A light not of this world covered his face. Aaron and Miriam came to stand beside him. The people gathered around, waiting for him to speak.

"With your own eyes you have seen God work miracles and wonders for you," Moses said. He paused, allowing memory to place images in their minds.

"God is more than power," Moses continued. "He is loving-kindness. His wish is for you to be like him. To imitate him. He offers you a way to do so."

The people fidgeted. They were going to be asked to do something.

Moses continued.

"He has asked me to place before you Ten Pathways," he said. "If you accept them and agree to make them your way, he will come down on the mount in three days to meet you and claim you for his own. He will be your God, and you will be his people."

Adding no word, subtracting none, as he had been commanded to do, Moses set forth the pathways. Before the people had a chance to ask what God would do for them in return, Moses repeated God's promise to send them rain and to assure them good crops, ending with the words, "You will be safe in your homes, for I will keep enemies away from your door."

A murmur passed through the crowd.

"What is the whispering?" Moses asked.

Miriam leaned over to her brother. "They have a question, Moses," she said.

"You have taught us that God is invisible," someone called. "How can an invisible God keep enemies away from our door?"

Moses would have liked to rebuke the questioner. Had God's great power not freed them from slavery? Had God not protected them till now? But Moses restrained himself. The Holy One was patient. He, too, must imitate God. He, too, must learn patience.

"You saw God work wonders to bring you out of Egypt, but did you see God?" he asked.

The people were silent.

"You see God rain down manna for you each morning, but do you see God?"

Observing that the people were attentive, Moses continued.

"You see God bring on the night and bring day from darkness, and little by little spread light throughout the world until it bursts into shining glory. Again and again you see light and darkness come and go, come and go. You see God do all this, but do you see God?"

The people, in the grip of wonderment, answered, "Tell God we will accept."

12

The Blue Flame

When three days had passed, the people left their tents and went out to meet God. Family after family, they set out for the foot of the mount, where Moses waited. They did not know what to expect. Moses had tried to prepare them to meet God, but they were not ready for the unnatural strangeness of the day that greeted them.

"What is this noise, this trembling earth?" the people asked one another.

From early morning, deep rumblings had sounded from the mount. Lights flashed there, and thunder cracked. Overhead, a dark cloud swirled, growing ever thicker, ever darker, shutting out the sun. It was not yet noon, and they walked in darkness, taking slow, grudging steps. Not because they could not see, but because they were afraid.

The angels were mystified. Why were the Israelites hanging back? They had made Moses' life miserable, demanding proof of God's existence. Now that they were on the way to meet God, they were dragging their feet, not rushing forward. The angels knew no greater happiness than to be in God's presence. They longed for him, as a thirsty deer yearns for water.

Moses waited for the Israelites to reach the foot of the mount. When they arrived, he drew a line in the sand with his sandal.

"Do not step beyond this line," he warned.

The people had no intention of crossing the line. They were frightened, already too close for comfort.

All at once the day stood still. The universe held its breath. No bird sang, no leaf stirred, no ox lowed, no creature uttered a sound as the Shekina, separating herself from the whole of Glory, descended with her escort of twenty-two thousand glowing angels, spreading a curtain of Glory under the sky. Celestial flames settled on the mount. Over their burning brightness hovered the blue flame of the Shekina.

With a voice like the rush of great waters, the Shekina said, "I am the Lord your God who brought you out of Egypt to be your God. You shall have no other gods beside me."

The people were too frightened to listen. Moving in a stupor, drifting back from the mount, they pleaded with Moses. "Let God speak to you, as before, and you speak to us," they begged.

The Shekina descends.

The blue flame vanished from the Israelites' sight, as the Shekina remained speaking to Moses.

As she spoke, he repeated her words to the people, saying:

"I am the Lord your God who brought you out of Egypt to be your God.

"You shall have no other gods beside me.

"Do not make false vows in my name.

"Remember the Sabbath day to keep it holy.

"Honor your father and mother.

"Do not murder.

"Do not commit adultery.

"Do not steal.

"Do not tell lies.

"Do not crave your neighbor's possessions."

The people, relieved that the meeting was over, said with one voice, "We will do and obey."

13

The Shekina Calms Hearts

The Israelites had wanted for nothing as they wandered in the wilderness. They had robes to cover their bodies and sandals for their feet. Baker angels rained down manna each morning, enough for every family. And the Miriam Well rolled along with them, going where they went, halting when they halted, providing them and their animals with water.

At day's end they made camp and ate. When they had put their little ones to sleep, the people gathered outside their tents, took places around the fire, and sat listening to Moses, Aaron, and Miriam teach about God.

"How can we know God?" they asked.

"With your heart," Miriam answered.

"With your eyes," Aaron said.

"With both you can only begin to get some idea," Moses said, "but you can never know God."

He continued. "We have no words, no language, to speak of God. He is too different. He made us, and made a world of marvels and wonders—sky, land, water, creatures. By these things, his handiwork—only by them can we know him. Only by his acts can we know his power."

"Aaron," someone called. "You tell us that God wants us to be holy. But what is holy?"

"Being good," Miriam said.

"What is good?"

"To be kind and helpful to others," she explained. "Especially to widows, orphans, and people in need. And to your animals," she added.

"When you have clean hands and a pure heart, you are holy," Aaron said.

Moses knew they wondered about the meaning of "clean hands." He answered before anyone could ask.

"Hurt no one, tell no lie, do no wrong, and you will have clean hands and a pure heart," he said.

He and Aaron and Miriam had repeated to the Israelites the Ten Pathways again and again. But the people could not grasp the idea of the seventh day. They always had questions about the pathway that said *"Remember the Sabbath day to keep it holy."*

Again someone brought up the matter. "How does a person remember a day? And how does one keep it holy?"

Moses had answered the question many times before, saying that when the Israelites rest on the seventh day, as God did, they keep the day as God had kept it. And when they praise God for creating wonders and marvels, they remember the day that God finished making the world.

This night he did not answer as before. Instead he said, "Tomorrow, at nightfall, is the start of the seventh day. Gather up a double portion of manna in the morning, so you need not work when the Sabbath comes. Prepare your patties and herbs. What you wish to bake, bake. What you wish to cook, cook. Let us all keep and remember the Sabbath together."

Angel Raziel, outside the Holy Curtain, and the other angels had been listening and were delighted with the idea.

"Angels," Raziel said. "I cannot leave my station, but you can. I cannot tell you what to do. But if I were able to leave, I would go down and sweeten their Sabbath for them."

Seven bands of angels flapped their wings in agreement and went down. They turned themselves into winds and swept the desert floor. They scented the air with the aroma of baking bread, savory herbs, and jasmine, so that when darkness fell and the Israelites came from their tents with their pots of food, they were able to seat themselves on a clean desert floor, as at a fine table, and enjoy the pleasing scents that filled the air.

Moses, Miriam, Aaron, and their families joined them.

The Israelite camp.

All sat together, watching the sky. And when they glimpsed the first three stars, signaling the arrival of a new day, Aaron welcomed the Sabbath, saying, "Praise God."

As he had taught them to do, the people answered, "Praise God to whom all praise is due."

The Shekina, separating herself from the whole of Glory, came down and brushed by each one, thus banishing worry and care from every heart. And as the moon beamed down on them, the Israelites sat with glad hearts, speaking in soft tones, listening to Miriam tell how people link themselves to God when they share the Sabbath with their maker.

"There are yet other links," Miriam said. "Each wonder we have here on earth is linked to a wonder in heaven. Earth is a copy of heaven." And she sang to them:

"If earth were a pond,
an eye would trace
pavilions of heaven
in her mirror face."

When all had eaten and drunk and were satisfied, Moses called the meal to an end, saying, "We thank you and bless you, king of the universe, who nourishes the entire world and arranges food for all his creatures."

The Holy One, looking down from heaven, was greatly pleased. The Heavenly Choir sang with surpassing sweetness, *"Praise him, all his angels, praise him sun and moon."* And each and every element of creation did so, each in its own voice. The earth hummed, the seas roared, the fields clapped, the trees sang, and all creatures made joyful noises.

14

Miriam and the Well Are Gone

The Israelites wandered on in the wilderness, now walking, now resting, now putting up their tents, now taking them down. Elders aged, little ones became children, children became young people who walked about the camp casting sly glances at the occupants of neighboring tents, looking for suitable mates. And a day came in the passage of time when Miriam died.

A great weeping went up from the Israelite camp. Heaven was also greatly saddened. The angels in charge of grasses came down to weep. The grasses wept with them. And wept also for themselves. For who would now hear their song?

When the people finished mourning, they realized that the Miriam Well had disappeared. They were alarmed. Their source of water was gone. The rock that had accompanied them throughout their wandering was no more. They went to speak to Moses and found him still mourning, still weeping.

"How long will you sit here and weep?" they asked.

"Shall I not weep for my sister?" Moses said.

"Weep also for us," they said. "For the Miriam Well that gave us water is gone. We will die of thirst. Our animals will die with us."

"Have no fear . . ." Moses began.

The people did not let him finish. They knew the end of the phrase: "God will provide." They did not want to hear words. They wanted a solution. They began to argue.

"Why did you take us out of Egypt and bring us to this barren desert?" they said. "A place without seed, without figs or vines or pomegranates. A place without water. Are you trying to kill us?"

Moses turned away, helpless before their complaints. He went to speak to Aaron, but his brother had nothing to suggest. The two prayed for help, and God heard them.

"Take your rod and go with the people among the rocks and stones of the desert," God said. "Tell them you will get water for them from a new rock. Let them choose the rock. Then raise your rod over it, and ask the rock for water. When they see water come from the rock, they will know that I am with them."

Moses did as God said. He took his rod inscribed with God's secret name and went out with Aaron into the desert wilderness.

The people saw the rod and took heart. This was the sacred rod. It would bring results. Confident, they took empty water skins to fill and went out with their little ones and animals, following Moses and Aaron among the rocks and stones of the desert. Moses passed rock after rock without acting. Walking along and walking along, the people became impatient.

"Try this rock," they said.

Now, when they said that, Moses should have held the rod over the rock, as God had told him to do. Instead he said, "Not this one," and walked on, Aaron beside him.

"Try this rock," the people said with growing anger.

"I will draw water where I will draw it," Moses said, walking on.

The people were ready to throw stones at him. "We are parched," they said. "Our little ones crave water. Our animals are dying. And you stroll leisurely through the desert."

Moses struck a rock in anger, and drops of water trickled out.

Despite their distress, the people broke out in laughter. "Not enough even for two infants," they said.

Enraged by their taunts, Moses struck the rock with force. Great quantities of water gushed out. The people ran to drink. They brought their little ones to the water, then their animals, and filled their empty water skins. Then all returned to camp.

Moses strikes the rock in anger.

In the quiet of the night, the Holy One, displeased, spoke to Moses.

"Moses," he said, "I told you to let the people choose the rock."

"They were growing disrespectful. I had to show them who was leader," Moses said.

"I told you to speak to the rock, and yet you struck it."

"They tried my patience," Moses said.

"You are their leader. A leader may not become impatient," the Holy One said.

"They were ready to stone me," said Moses.

"They were desperate and spoke from distress," the Holy One said. "No one is responsible for words spoken in distress."

"I could not hold back my anger," Moses said.

"Their concern was for their little ones and their animals," the Holy One said. "I value more their loving-kindness than your temper."

Moses fell silent. He had given offense.

"Because you have disobeyed me, you will not enter the Promised Land," God said. "Neither you nor Aaron."

The pronouncement upset Moses greatly. He could not yet speak for himself. But why should Aaron be punished? "Aaron only accompanied me," he said. "He has done nothing."

"For that will he be punished," God said. "He heard my instructions. He raised neither his voice nor his hand to stop you."

Moses' heart was in a tumult. *Could it be? Was he not to enter the Promised Land?* Was the event for which he had been preparing for forty years to be denied him?

As he thought about the matter, he found reasons to reverse his thoughts and rekindle hope for himself. Was not the Holy One goodness? Was he not kindness? And mercy? Was he not patient and forgiving? Moses' pain eased as he assured himself that God would forgive him when the time came, that he would relent. For God was merciful.

15

Eighty Thousand Youths Named Aaron

Hardly had the pain of losing Miriam left when Moses' brother Aaron died, opening anew Moses' wounds of mourning.

Aaron was greatly beloved by the people. More so even than Moses. While Moses made demands on them and scolded them when they misbehaved, Aaron spoke gently to them. His manner was kindly. His one wish was for peace—between person and person, tribe and tribe. For people to love one another.

If he learned that two were angry at each other, he rushed to make peace. To this one he said, "How your friend misses you! With what loving words the friend speaks of you!" To the other he said the same. Ceaselessly, he went back and forth between the two with words of warmth and friendship until they fell weeping into each other's arms, glad to see each other again.

So much did the people love Aaron that almost every family had named a son for him.

Thus it was that when the people went to bury Aaron, eighty thousand boys named Aaron poured from their tents weeping, mourning their loss. "The peacemaker is gone," they cried, walking along with Aaron's bier overhead. The angels in charge of mourning had come down to prepare Aaron for burial themselves. It was they who carried the bier aloft, singing softly to themselves, "He walked in peace and uprightness and turned many away from evil deeds."

Moses was inconsolable. Gone from his side were the sister and brother of his youth. "Woe is me, who am now left alone!" he cried. "I buried my sister and brother, but who will bury me? Who will weep for me?"

There was an answer, but Moses did not hear it. In heaven, the Holy One said to the angels, "He need not fear. I myself shall bury him."

16

Moses Pleads for Himself

After the long years of wandering, of parents dying and children growing up to become parents themselves, Moses and the Israelites arrived at the river Jordan. On the other side of the water lay Canaan: the land God had promised to their ancestors. The people spread out along the banks of the river, gazing across in quiet joy, heedless of the soft rain that had begun to fall.

The angels, looking on, were glad for them. But their hearts broke for Moses. He would not be crossing over with the others. He knew this. He had heard it before. "Moses," the Holy One had said, "you will not cross over." The words were clear. But Moses had persuaded himself otherwise, telling himself again and again, "The Holy One will relent."

Now, the Holy One knew Moses' heart. And knew of Moses' belief that the thing would not come to pass. And as the rain continued to fall lightly on the banks of the river Jordan, the Holy One repeated the words for the last time.

"Moses," he said.

"I am here," Moses answered.

"The people will cross over, but you will not."

Moses' heart fainted. He could not accept the judgment, and began to plead for himself.

"Dear and Holy One," he said. "When you told me this before, you were speaking to a leader, a prophet. I beg you, take away my high position. Name someone else as leader. Let me enter the land as a common man."

"It cannot be, Moses," the Holy One said. "I have decreed it. Ya'asriel has already written in the pages of the book that you will not enter."

Moses was disconsolate. An entry in the book by the celestial engraver could not be changed.

Still . . . perhaps after all. . . . Again he tried.

"Dear and Holy One," he said. "You have set me over an unruly people. I have tamed them for you and made them into a wise and understanding people. I have taught them to love you. Other nations say, *Fortunate is the God whose people this is.*"

"I have done as much and more for you, Moses," the Holy One said. "I have brought you up to heaven to meet my angels. Only you know my secret name. Be comforted, for I have ordered Ya'asriel also to write in the book the words 'Only Moses has spoken to me face to face.'"

Moses could find no joy in the words. He had reached the end. Even so, he could not stop.

"Dear and Holy One," he said. "You are now seated on your throne of justice. I beg you, rise up and move to your throne of mercy."

"Enough, Moses," the Holy One said. "You will not enter."

Moses heaved a great sigh. "Woe to my feet that may not enter the land," he sobbed. "Woe to my hands that may not pluck fruit from its trees. Woe to my tongue that may not taste the milk and honey that flow there."

"Refrain your voice from weeping and your eyes from tears," the Holy One said.

"I beg of you, let me at least see the land," Moses said.

"Come up to the top of Mount Nebo, which is opposite Jericho, and I will show you the land."

The fine rain that had been falling stopped, giving way to a rainbow. And the golden aura of the Shekina appeared and presented Moses with a cloud. "Use it as a shield as you go up," she said.

Protecting himself with the cloud, Moses rose up. When he reached the top of the mount, the Holy One drew aside the curtain of time, revealing the dazzling brilliance of the first light he had created.

By its great brightness Moses could see the entire world, could see past, present, and future all at once. He could see spread across Canaan, the Promised

Land, Israelite tents standing side by side in orderly rows, like gardens along the river, like so many aloes planted by God. And see invading armies lay waste to the land and bring it to ruin. And the land grow calm again, and Israelite families dwelling in safety, each with its own grapevine, each with a fig tree of its own.

17

Moses Does Not Want to Die

As Moses came down from the mount, Micha'el, his guardian angel, said in his ear, "Do you know what tomorrow is?"

Moses did know.

"It is your birth day, the seventh day of the twelfth month," she said. "You were born at noon."

Moses did not want to be reminded.

"You have one more day to live," she said.

Moses knew his life was at an end. He had learned many secrets on his visits to heaven. The angels had taught him that a child, when it is born, is allotted so many years of life on Earth. The child is also given a soul. Moses' allotted time on Earth was one hundred and twenty years. Tomorrow at noon his lifespan would end.

He did not want to die.

"Dear and Holy One—" he began.

"One day more, Moses," the Holy One said, not letting him finish.

"I beg you, let me stay in this world," Moses said.

"Everyone born must die. That is the law of life."

"Please make an exception of me," Moses said.

"Noon tomorrow—"

"Let me live," Moses pleaded.

"If I let you live, people will begin to worship you and forget about me," the Holy One said.

Moses' face burned with shame. Beside God, what was he? A leaf that dries up and disappears? Smoke that vanishes? Even so, he could not stop pleading.

"Dear and Holy One," he said. "Take away my human form and let me be an animal that eats grass. Let me be a bird that flies about and finds its own food. Only let me stay in this world."

"You have said enough, Moses."

Aware that words had failed him, Moses tried prayer. He had visited heaven and knew how to enter the Gates of Prayer. Drawing a circle around himself, he began, "Blessed is God, creator of the world—"

His words were never heard. As Moses opened his mouth to speak, the Holy One had called to Abraziel, the gatekeeper, "Seal the gates." Akraziel, the celestial herald, hearing the gates snap shut, sent down angels Zakun and Lahash to snatch the words from Moses' lips.

Angel Raziel felt sorry for Moses. His end had come. Nothing could change that.

"You have already said too much, Moses," the Holy One said. "It is time for you to die."

With his life force draining away, with little breath left to link him to the breath of God in the universe, Moses began to mourn for himself.

As he faded, it was time for his soul to leave his body and return to heaven. But Moses' soul failed to appear. She had to leave before he could die.

"Gabriel," the Holy One said, "go and bring his soul."

"I cannot do it, Holy One," Gabriel said. "He has been my student and friend."

The Holy One understood the archangel's refusal.

"Micha'el, you go," the Holy One said.

Micha'el could hardly speak for the tears in her eyes. "I have been his guardian from the time he was a babe in Egypt. How can I go?" she said.

"Send me," called a familiar voice.

"It is the Alien," Raziel said.

Satan had been waiting for this moment. He had always been jealous of Moses and hated him. And hated Micha'el for the love she bore Moses. How often heaven had heard Satan singing, "When Micha'el's eyes fill with tears, my mouth will fill with laughter."

"Let me do it," Satan said.

"Begone, evil one," the Holy One said. "I shall attend to the matter myself."

The Holy One's answer delighted Raziel.

18

Ya

The angels came to watch. It had never happened before that a soul refused to leave a body. They were sorry to see Moses sitting, distressed, near death and unable to die because his soul would not leave.

The Shekina took the matter into her own hands. In the holy storehouse in the fourth heaven was the scepter that God had used when he made the world. The Shekina separated herself from the whole of Glory, removed the scepter, and with it went down with angels Micha'el and Gabriel and four bands of escort angels on either side of her.

When her golden Glory settled over Moses, the escort angels stood with softly beating wings around him, forming a fence of love. Micha'el and Gabriel, on either side of Moses, touched their wings together, forming a pillow, and gently lowered his head to the ground.

The Shekina, hovering over Moses, said, "Close your eyes, friend."

Moses did so.

"Fold your hands on your chest."

Moses did so.

She placed the holy scepter on his chest, ordering his soul to leave his body. The soul did not stir.

The Shekina spoke to the soul. "My daughter," she said, "you must leave him, so he can die."

"I cannot leave him," the soul said.

"You must."

"I love him and wish to stay with him."

"Your time in his body is over," the Shekina said. "Come, return to heaven. Your place is there, with the other holy souls."

"Do not ask it of me," the soul said. "I beg you."

Moses heard her and was moved by her words. He could not allow her to do this to herself. A soul that does not leave a body faces misery and desolation, roaming the earth forever, going from graveyard to graveyard, looking for a body that no longer exists. He could not let her face such a future.

"Go, please," he said to her. "I will rot away, and then where will you be?"

"Moses, how can I leave you?" the soul said.

"Do it for my sake," Moses said.

"There is no other way," the Shekina said to the soul.

Moses' soul returns to heaven.

Sorrowfully, slowly, sobbing, the soul left Moses' body.

"Ya," Moses said with his last breath.

The Shekina placed a kiss on Moses' lips as burial angels came with joy and beaming faces, singing, "Enter into peace." And singing, the angels accompanied the Shekina as she rose up with the soul and brought her to the Palace of Love, a secret room in heaven occupied by radiant souls.

The pining soul sorrowed a moment longer, then began to rejoice with the other souls, for it was here that the Holy One came to chat with souls, and kiss them, when the behavior of humans disappointed him.

Notes

The stories in this book are based on the biblical passages and legends indicated below. The two strands have been woven together to retell a popular Bible legend. Dialogue and descriptive detail have been added for narrative flow.

Treating Raziel and Micha'el as female angels is based on references in books of Jewish mysticism, which speak of male and female angels. These texts also refer to wisdom as one of God's qualities, and speak of wisdom in the feminine. They also speak of the Shekina as God's female presence on earth.

Angel songs are adaptations of psalms and Jewish prayers, unless otherwise noted.

Attributions to M.C. refer to inventions of the author.

Introduction

From the Bible:

Let us make humans. Genesis 1:26.

Angels: Appear to Abraham. Genesis 18:2./Two come to Sodom. Genesis 19:1./Walk to and fro. Zechariah 1:10./God's servants. Psalm 103:20–21./Singers. Isaiah 6:3./Seraphim. Isaiah 6:1./Guardians. Exodus 32:34./He will give his angels charge over you. Psalm 91:11./The Lord shall preserve you. Psalm 121:7–8.

Heaven: The heavens were opened and I saw visions of God. Ezekiel 1:2./The court was full of the brightness of the Lord's glory. Ezekiel 10:4./A paved work of sapphire stone. Exodus 24:10.

Links: I am your God. Ezekiel 34:31./Heaven is my throne. Isaiah 66:1./God is king of all the earth. Psalm 47:6–8./The Lord looked down. Psalm 14:2./Guardian angels, as above, among angels./God is God above and below. Deuteronomy 4:39./All in heaven and earth is yours. I Chronicles 29:11.

Books written on earth: God commands prophets to write. Isaiah 8:1, Jeremiah 30:2./Commands Moses, "Write this. . . ." Exodus 17:14./Write you this song. Deuteronomy 31:19.

Books written in heaven: Whoever sins against me, I will blot him out of my book. Exodus 32:33./Blot me out of your book. Exodus 32:32.

Midrash and Legend: Turn it and turn it. *Sayings of the Fathers,* 5:25./Ya'asriel and the angels./Seven heavens./Each blade of grass. Rabbi Nachman of Bratslav.

Chapter 1 • The Sacred Rod

From the Bible:

The rod. Exodus 4:2./I am slow of speech. Exodus 4:10./The bush burned with fire. Exodus 3:2./Is there not Aaron, your brother? Exodus 4:14.

From Legend:

Rod inscribed with God's secret name.

Chapter 2 • The World Above, the World Below

From the Bible:

Heaven was full of the brightness of the Lord's glory. Ezekiel 10:4./As the color of electrum (amber). Ezekiel 1:4./Holy, holy, holy is the Lord. Isaiah 6:3./Praise him, all his angels. Psalm 148:2./None shall see me and live. Exodus 33:20./And all the sons of God shouted (sang) for joy. Job 38:7.

From Legend:

The color of Glory is amber./The seven heavens./Ya'asriel./God is hidden behind the Holy Curtain./The Heavenly Chorus.

Chapter 3 • Gifts in the Wilderness

From the Bible:

I will send an angel before you. Exodus 33:2./I will rain bread from heaven for you. Exodus 16:4./The bread of angels. Psalm 78:25./And the cloud of the Lord was over them. Numbers 10:34./They [angels] had human hands under their wings. Ezekiel 1:8.

From Legend:

Israel received three gifts in the wilderness: the well, shade, and manna. Angels: Spread a cloud over them./Swept the desert floor./The deadly snake./ He makes new angels./Manna, mill, miller, angels bake./Manna's various tastes./A movable well.

Chapter 4 • The Miriam Well

From the Bible:

Spring up, O well. Numbers 21:17./Miriam the prophet took a timbrel in her hand. Exodus 15:20./Praise him with timbrel and dance, praise him with lute and pipe. Psalm 150:4.

From Legend:

God wrought the miracle of the rock well for the goodness of Miriam./All the herbs in the earth, to which angels have been assigned, have a mystery of their own./Every blade of grass has its own guardian angel./The song of the grasses. Adaptation of a poem by Rabbi Nachman of Bratslav./Miriam could hear the song. M.C.

Chapter 5 • By the Mouth of the Cloud

From the Bible:

And Moses entered into the midst of a cloud. Exodus 24:18./He will give his angels charge over you. Psalm 91:11./What is man that you should be mindful of him? Psalm 8:5. (Stories about jealous and troublesome angels grow out of this psalm.)/And Enoch was no more, for God took him. Genesis 5:24./Enter his gates with thanksgiving. Psalm 100:4.

The Shekina: The idea of God's female presence on earth is derived from two Bible passages: Let them make me a sanctuary, that I may dwell among you. Exodus 25:8; I will walk among you. Leviticus 26:12.

From Legend:

Enoch/Metatron, prince of the Face./Metatron is a link between the Divine and the human./The Holy One made Moses like an angel./Moses' visits to heaven./Forty-nine gates of wisdom./A blinding spark./God made ten descents to earth in the form of the Shekina./Moses could feel her breath on the back of his neck. M.C.

Chapter 6 • Angel Raziel

From the Bible:

The Lord spoke to Moses face to face. Exodus 33:11./I will be your God, and you will be my people. Leviticus 26:12./Ten Commandments. Exodus, 20:2–14./The paths [are] a tree of life for those who grasp it. . . . Its ways are ways of pleasantness. All its paths are peace. Proverbs 3:17–18./And I will give grass in your fields for your cattle, and you shall eat and be satisfied. Deuteronomy 11:15./And I will betroth you unto me. Hosea 2:21./Add no word. Deuteronomy 4:2.

From Legend:

Raziel sits outside the Holy Curtain.

Chapter 7 • Moses Silences the Angels

From the Bible:

A soft answer turns away wrath. Proverbs 15:1.

From Legend:

The angels confront Moses./The paths are not for them./In heaven, night shines as day./The mouth of the cloud.

Chapter 8 • Something Entirely New

From the Bible:

I will do marvels such as have not been seen. Exodus 34:10.

From Legend:

Five hundred years to walk across heaven./Singing with lips. M.C./ Something entirely new is about to happen./Aliens, demonic forces that torment humans./God had employed Satan elsewhere on purpose.

Chapter 9 • The Mountains Argue

From the Bible:

Why do you look askance, you mountain peaks, at the mount that God desired? Psalm 68:17./Before honor goes humility. Proverbs 15:33./The man Moses was very meek. Numbers 12:3./Walk humbly with your God. Micah 6:8.

From Legend:

The mounts argue./Torah given on Sinai because (1) God loves the humble; and (2) it is located in no man's land, and no one can say it is not for us.

Chapter 10 • Satan Tries to Interfere

From the Bible:

Satan stood up against Israel. 1 Chronicles 21:1.

From Legend:

Satan, a former good angel./God employed Satan elsewhere./Raziel thought the Holy One went too far. M.C./You had to keep proving your power so they would not say, "God cannot do it."/They act according to their natures./ I know they worshiped rams in Egypt: I put them there.

Chapter 11 • But Do You See God?

From the Bible:

The Lord will come down in the sight of the people. Exodus 19:11./I will be your God, and you will be my people. Leviticus 26:12./And I will betroth you unto me. Hosea 2:21./He fills heaven and earth, but you cannot see him. Jeremiah 23:24.

From Legend:

God is goodness./But did you see God?/He [the Shekina, God's female earth presence] will walk among you.

Chapter 12 • The Blue Flame

From the Bible:

And the Lord came down upon Mount Sinai. Exodus 19:20./Heaven and earth will witness this treaty. Deuteronomy 32:1./As the hart pants after the water brooks, so pants my soul after you, O God. Psalm. 42:2./He stretched out the heavens as a curtain. Isaiah 40:22./Let not God speak. Exodus 20:16./All that God has spoken we will do. Exodus 19:8./Ten Commandments. Exodus 20:14.

From Legend:

What is this noise?/Angels spread a curtain of Glory./One of the ten descents made by the Shekina./Universe held its breath./Flame angels./The blue around flame represents the Shekina./No bird chirped, etc./The brilliance of the Shekina, her radiance went forth.

Chapter 13 • The Shekina Calms Hearts

From the Bible:

Your clothes are not waxen old upon you, and your shoe is not waxen old upon your foot. Deuteronomy 29:4./You shall keep my Sabbaths, for a sign between me and you . . . and [it is] holy to the Lord. Exodus 31:13./Who has clean hands and a pure heart. Psalm 24:4./What you wish to bake, bake. Exodus 16:23./You shall eat and be satisfied, and you shall bless your God for the good land that he gave you. Deuteronomy 8:10./God loves the study of Torah [the paths] . . . for by study comes the knowledge of the will of God. Paraphrase of Proverbs 2:5./Let the earth rejoice. Psalm 96:11.

From Legend:

Angels sweep the desert floor./Baking and savory herbs in the air. M.C./The Shekina enters the palace of time on Friday at sunset./Whirligigs and demons disappear./Moses composed the grace after meals./Everything in the world below corresponds with the world above./Miriam's song. Adapted by M.C. from legend that God modeled the earth on the pattern of heaven.

Chapter 14 • Miriam and the Well Are Gone

From the Bible:

And Miriam died . . . and there was no water. Numbers 20:1–2./Speak unto the rock. Numbers 20:8./Moses smote the stone twice. Numbers 20:11./You sanctified me not in the eyes of the people. Numbers 20:12./A righteous person takes care of his beasts. Proverbs 12:10./Goodness, mercy, patience as attributes of God. Exodus 34:6.

From Legend:

The well gave water as long as Miriam lived./Angels of mourning came down to weep./Grasses weep. M.C./Drops of water trickle from the rock./The Holy One forgives words uttered in distress./A divinely appointed leader may not become impatient with people.

Chapter 15 • Eighty Thousand Youths Named Aaron

From the Bible:

Aaron died in Mount Hor. Deuteronomy. 32:50./He walked in peace and uprightness. Malachi 2:6./Seek peace and pursue it. Psalm 34:15.

From Legend:

Eighty thousand youths named Aaron./The peacemaker is gone./The angels prepared Aaron for burial./His bier floating in the air./Moses laments, "Woe is me!"/I myself will bury you.

Chapter 16 • Moses Pleads for Himself

From the Bible:

God knows the secrets of the heart. Psalm 44:22./A wise and understanding people. Deuteronomy 4:6./With him do I speak mouth to mouth. Numbers

12:8./God reveals to Moses his secret name. Exodus 6:2./Refrain your voice from weeping. Jeremiah 31:16./Write this for a record in the book. Exodus 17:14./Show us your kindness. Psalm 85:8./Moses went up to Mount Nebo. Deuteronomy 34:1./As aloes planted by the Lord. Numbers 24:6./Each family under their own fig tree. l Kings 5:5.

From Legend:

Moses pleads for himself./You have set me over an unruly people./Two thrones, justice and mercy./Angel Ya'asriel./Rainbow, a mystical name for the Shekina./By means of the first light [Adam] could gaze from one end of the universe to the other./Like gardens along the river./Moses saw the future.

Chapter 17 • Moses Does Not Want to Die

From the Bible:

Take me not away in the midst of my days. Psalm 102:25./Wild asses live in the wilderness and eat grass. Job 6:5./Out of the depths have I called to thee. Psalm 130:1./A book of remembrance was written. Malachi 3:16./Who can live and not see death? Psalm 89:49./He will give his angels charge over you. Psalm 91:11.

From Legend:

Though the Holy One is long-suffering, he will exact payment./Moses does not want to die./Micha'el [Moses' guardian angel] and Gabriel do not want to go down./Moses draws a circle around himself./Lock all gates./Angels snatch the words from Moses' mouth./Satan waits for Micha'el to weep./The Holy One will attend to the matter himself.

Chapter 18 • Ya

From the Bible:

Moses was 120 years old when he died. Deuteronomy 34:7./And the spirit will return to God who gave it. Ecclesiastes 12:7./And his soul shall mourn over him. Job 14:22./To this day Moses' burial place remains unknown. Deuteronomy 34:6./There has never been a prophet in Israel as great as Moses. Deuteronomy 34:10.

From Legend:

Moses' soul refused to leave./Moses died on Sabbath afternoon./On Moses' chest God placed the scepter he used when he created the world./Angels make a pillow of wings. M.C./Ya, (one of the names of God), as a last breath. M.C./Angels came joyously./The soul was returned to the Palace of Love.

Source Books Consulted
and Drawn Upon

Abelson, J. *Jewish Mysticism: An Introduction to the Kabbalah*. New York: Sepher-Hermon Press, third edition, 1981.

Ginzberg, Louis. *Legends of the Jews*. Philadelphia: The Jewish Publication Society of America, 1992.

Goldin, Judah, trans. *The Fathers According to Rabbi Nathan*. New Haven & London: Yale Univ. Press, 1955.

Kushner, Lawrence. *Honey from the Rock*. Woodstock, Vt: Jewish Lights, 1990.

Matt, Daniel C. *The Essential Kabbalah: The Heart of Jewish Mysticism*. San Francisco: Harper, 1955.

Patai, Raphael. *Gates to the Old City: A Book of Jewish Legends*. New York: Avon Books, 1980.

Rashi's Commentary. Pentateuch with Targum Onkelos, Haphtaroth. Translated and annotated by Rabbi A. K. Silbermann in collaboration with Rev. M. Rosenbaum. Jerusalem and New York: Feldheim Publishers, 1985.

Scholem, Gershom G., Editor. *Zohar: The Book of Splendor—Basic Reading from the Kabbalah.* New York: Schocken Books, Inc., 1963.

Miriam Chaikin was born in Jerusalem and grew up in Brooklyn, New York. She is the author of many prize-winning books of Jewish interest, including, for Clarion, *A Nightmare in History* and *Joshua in the Promised Land*. She lives in New York City and spends part of each year in Israel.

Alexander Koshkin has illustrated several books for Clarion, including *Atalanta's Race* by Shirley Climo and *Images of God* by John and Katherine Paterson. Mr. Koshkin is a graduate of the famed Surikov Art College in Moscow, where he makes his home.